Food on Their Table

A Dystopian Novelette

by Diane Morrison

Published by Diane Morrison

Aradia Enterprises
5583 Silver Star Rd.
Vernon, BC Canada V1B 3P7

© 2017 by Diane Morrison

The final approval for this material is granted by the author.

First electronic edition: May 2017
First print edition: June 2017

Printed in Canada & the United States.

ISBN 978-0-9959276-3-6

Printed in Times New Roman.

http://www.sablearadia.com
http://dianemorrison.wordpress.com

Acknowledgements

No writer truly writes alone. I would like to thank the Vernon Writer's Critique Group for helping me hone my craft. I would also like to thank the indie authors' community, especially the ladies of the Vegas Fight Club, for being so supportive. Most of all, I would like to thank my partner and editor Jamie for his hard work and his bravery in taking me on, and my husband Erin for his unrelenting love and support.

Dedication

For my dad, for encouraging his weird daughter to be herself.

Table of Contents

Habitat

The parched surface of the burnt-out planet thirsts. Yellow dust blows over the cracked desert landscape, scouring mountains and ruins alike. Overhead, thick cloud makes a truth of an ancient prophecy; the sun is as black as sackcloth, the moon has turned to blood.

The land is yellow dust and craggy rock, empty in some places for thousands of miles. But every so often, usually in the higher elevations, one finds evidence that it may not always have been so. Towering structures of glass and steel still rise like accusatory fingers from the dust and stone, though most of the glass is scoured opaque, blind white eyes staring into an empty world. Some lie in fallen, twisted heaps, the bones of monsters.

In some places, one can even find worn wood desiccating in the merciless heat, over time transforming from something living and organic into grey stone. There is little sign other than this that trees once spread their leafy branches over vast stretches of this desolate world. They are not even a memory.

In some places, endless fields and mountains of salt roll on for thousands of miles. Eventually they descend into a murky saline abyss. Water is desperately needed, but nothing lives here. This water is poison.

Yet the rhythmic grind of a churning engine runs on and on, although one must to be right on top of it to notice it under the endless scream of the droning wind. A giant industrial complex houses an enormous pump and filtration system. It is sucking up hundreds of gallons of the saline at once, which is then flushed through a series of underground filters. One can see that the salt is eventually spit back out in a thick grey sludge, and maybe this sludge is contributing to the salt residue. But the water disappears.

Where does the water go? Like thousands of other systems of its kind, the pumping station flushes fresh water into an expansive underground, interconnected system of pipes. The pipes eventually join up into an enormous water main. From there, the pipes drop the water several miles underground.

Giant cisterns collect this water in tremendous pools, and those pools are now drained by yet more pipes. If one were to follow one of them, eventually it would open out to a series of interconnected rooms. These rooms are illuminated with bright violet-white light, a blinding contrast to the darkness of the tunnels. One would eventually realize that one had arrived at a kind of farm. There are thousands, perhaps millions, of vegetables, and occasionally herbs, growing in neat, long rows of boxes. The vegetables are gravid and swollen, and there are extra roots, fruits and limbs extending from the plants.

After the vegetables come monumental chambers braced and bolstered by columns of metal and stone. Other than the watering system and the fluorescent lights, one might think these are grassy fields. In a way, one would be correct. These are grain fields – wheat, barley, millet, and also cotton and flax, though these with much shorter plants than one might expect. There is an airlock separating each of these chambers, and a complex system that carefully controls heat and humidity.

After the airlocks, one finds little groves in even bigger chambers. 'Ah, *here* are the trees!' one might think to oneself. Here are orchards of miniaturized fruit trees, except that they produce enough equally-miniaturized fruits that their branches struggle against the weight.

Long rows of pipes run above the boxes and the tiny trees. The water one has followed from the surface does not feed them. Instead, looking closer, one realizes that the pipes that emerge from their long road to the outside feed water bottles in thousands of small cages. These cages house chickens, rabbits, and in some cases, large rats. Their droppings fall into ditches that run along the pathways between the boxes, where carp, goldfish, and similar bottom-feeders swim, next to columns of rice or sugar cane growing between.

That water is then pumped out of the farms, where it is blended with sewage water that has been treated with chemicals and then triple-filtered. This water is finally pumped through those overhead sprinkler systems to water the fields of grass and boxes. It only mists the trees; apparently, they are watered through a different system.

No ornamental grass is permitted here, nor is there a flower that cannot also be eaten. Instead, there is sand. Here one finally sees that yes, there are people, milling about in the indoor orchards. The light is allowed to be less white and purple here, because now it also serves the needs of human health. The people are reading on tablets and e-readers, or sitting on benches and chatting, or possibly they are playing metal and plastic instruments. Occasionally they are doing light exercise, yoga, or qi gong. No one is walking a dog, and there are no birds nor bees, though tiny mechanical drones seem to buzz between trees when they are in blossom.

The people do not pick the fruit. Such a crime is punishable by death.

Beneath a tree covered with tiny apples like pom-poms on a clown suit, a gangly youth is doodling on a tablet with a stylus.

He has never seen paper; indeed, cannot imagine it. He is drawing something he has no word for. It is a field of trees, thick trees, trees not planted in even rows. He has never seen such a thing, nor has anyone he knows. But someone has mentioned the idea to him, though when, he cannot remember. It has infected him with an eerie fascination.

He is neither short nor tall. There is little that stands out about his physical stature. His skin is an average shade of café-au-lait, and his eyes are dark brown. Perhaps one might suggest that his black-brown hair is a little overlong for the prescribed style, but that wouldn't even be an uncommon way for a youth to push the boundaries. He is neither thick nor thin, neither especially athletic nor slight of build. He is unusual in two ways that are not easy to see. The first is that he is unusually quiet. The second is his most closely-guarded secret.

He has spent most of his life trying not to attract the attention of the Hegemony, who control all that he knows and sees. But despite his best efforts, he has done so anyway.

His name is Paul. Today is his sixteenth birthday.

Supper

The eyes of the Hegemony are not all-seeing, but they see quite a bit. Their people are accustomed to cameras watching their every move and hidden microphones recording their every utterance. They communicate frequently over a vast computer network and they know that the Hegemony logs every key touched and every photo exchanged. Most of them don't worry about it much.

Paul understands the logic. There are so many people, why would the Hegemony care about any individual enough to sift through the mountain of data collected to concentrate on any one of them? Just don't create trouble, and trouble won't come to you.

Paul understands, but he knows better, because his mother thought the same thing, and she is gone now. Paul thinks that she's been killed, but he can't be sure. She vanished in the middle of the night. Two helmed men in the Gendarmerie came in the dark to bundle her into an aircar, and he never saw her again. His friends are sympathetic, but he knows that secretly, they believe she must have done something significant, and illegal, to get their attention. Nothing he can say will dissuade them.

He spent much of his time alone before that incident, anyway. He likes to read, and not just the Recommended Literature prescribed by the official school. Thousands, maybe millions of books have been scanned from the Time Before, and he is fascinated by them. He will read anything. He has learned much that most people do not know about the Time Before. Some of his friends don't even believe him.

His reading is interrupted by a blip on his tablet screen and a popup. Paul has been dreading messages today; he supposes that everyone must. He opens the popup, and it is indeed the notice that he has feared:

Paul Rand: Happy birthday! You are due to report to a licensed physician for your Assessment, which is mandatory for all sixteen-year-old Citizens. Please book your appointment in the next few days. Failure to do so may be viewed as Non-Compliance. Thank you for your cooperation.

Paul sighs and dismisses the window, then promptly conjures up a scheduling screen with his assigned physician. 15:00 hours on Thursday is the earliest she can see Paul. Paul books it and closes the window.

What will they find when they do the Assessment, Paul wonders? It is more than idle curiosity. The outcome will determine the course of his future.

He wonders what his friends are doing. Dmitri is probably still at work, he realizes when he checks the time. After his Assessment, which was three months ago, he started working in the vegetable farm. Nisaba, on the other hand, was approved for Advanced Sciences two months ago, and she is now studying to be a pathologist. Gurjit is studying to be an Engineer.

Will he keep in contact with his friends after Assessment? He's not certain. He knows that while Nisaba and Gurjit continue to correspond with him, they don't talk to Dmitri much anymore. He supposes it's only natural; what do budding scientists, who spend every waking moment studying, have in common with a farm labourer? Despite the Hegemony's urging that all jobs are of equal importance, and everyone contributes equally to the maintenance of the Habitat, he knows that there is an unspoken sense of stratification.

Paul is reading an ancient comedy about a man who hitchhikes around the galaxy. He's sure he doesn't get most of the jokes.

Another blip appears in the corner of his screen. Andrea. He sighs and opens it.

'What?'

'You have to come back now,' his least-favourite foster sister informs him pompously.

'Why?' He is defensive. He hates the group home where he lives. He hates the so-called 'foster parents' the most, but some of the other kids he could do without too. Like Andrea, who bullies the other kids but tattles if anyone is seen doing anything outside of regulations. Paul has a few old lash-scars from her 'dutiful reporting.'

'It's time for dinner,' she informs him in a far too-perfectly innocent voice.

'That's early,' he remarks, getting up from the ground and brushing the sand off his pants. He just looked at the time. It was only 16:30 a minute ago! But he realizes as he is checking this that he is wrong, it is 17:00, or so close to as to make no difference. Not that early, he supposes.

'We're waiting,' snaps Andrea as she swipes the screen and disappears.

Paul has no intention of keeping them. His stomach is growling already. It seems he is always hungry. He knows that he is greedy – everyone's food ration is calculated for required caloric intake, and as a teenager he already receives ten percent extra – but tell his stomach that! It goes on growling just the same.

He punches up an aircar via his tablet and one appears. He gets in and the bubble-shaped craft speeds through the long dark corridors that link the Farms to Education, then Recreation. This section houses the public gymnasium and the recreation park, which is full of people even at this hour, he can see through the plexiglass windows. There is a flash of brightness as they pass the full-spectrum lighting and artificial plants with hexagonal golden thread-patterns through their leaves. They convert the residual full-spectrum light back into energy and feed it to the rest of the Habitat for its use. They even contain real chlorophyll, Paul understands; but there's something uncanny about them, something that reminds you that they aren't *real*. He prefers to go out of his way to find real trees.

The aircar darkens again as they pass through the red-light district and the bars. One is limited to three drink tickets per week, but there is a thriving black-market trade in those. They can be spent on any sort of fermented beverage, from artificially-flavoured coolers and ciders to pure vodka, and some of the bars will even serve illegal hooch made from rye-stalks or fruit peels or chemical by-products or Founders know what else. Public drunkenness is illegal, but people will drag even the sorriest drunk in from the corridor and hide him in exchange for a few drink tickets of their own. The Gendarmerie knows this goes on, Paul is certain, but they have bigger fish to fry. Speaking of food.

The lithe and writhing sex workers in the next red-light radiating windows, however, are subject to strict Hegemonic regulation. This is one of the options if one is selected for Hospitality after Assessment, he understands, especially if one shows unusual flexibility and dexterity as well. Andrea claims that she would never choose such a profession rather loudly, but Paul thinks the lady doth protest too much.

Paul knows that the broadcasting stations are here somewhere also, but he isn't sure where. He wonders idly if the Habitat Orchestra is playing tonight, and if they will do Beethoven. He's fond of Beethoven, much less of Debussy or even Bach. Mozart has his high points, and Tchaikovsky is amazing, but the Hegemony discourages the Orchestra from playing too much of his work. Paul would love to hear the *1812 Overture* with the original cannons, but he knows that would never be approved. Besides, where would they find a cannon? They were all on the Surface, if there were any left out there in the ruins.

At last the aircar reaches the Residential District. Some decoration is permitted on individual doors, and most people have availed themselves of the statute to give themselves some form of originality – a door knocker or a small wreath, maybe a mural or a framed picture. Often, a family's most valuable possessions dangle from their front door. Why not? There's no crime, not with the corridor cameras and the Gendarmerie everywhere. And besides, how else was one to impress the neighbours?

They are divided by number of beds in the dwelling and assigned according to 'need' and 'merit.' But the Department of Housing is not interested in personal preferences. A family of four might find itself in a dwelling with four bunkbeds, and never mind that the parents are a married couple. He remembers that when he was a small child, his family had a dwelling like that, and his parents threw their mattresses on the floor and pushed them together in the living room, and he and his older brother Jamie shared the other bunk.

Paul's heart catches in his throat. He has not thought of Jamie much in the past couple of years, and this realization makes him feel guilty. Perhaps it's good that he's put that all behind him, but it can't help but be fresh in his mind with his own Assessment looming.

The aircar arrives at the foster home and dings to announce it has done so. Paul tries to get out but the door is locked. 'Please record your thumbprint,' a voice that might almost sound real, if it wasn't so oddly cheerful, requests. Impatiently he jabs his thumb in the slot and waits for the ding. When he hears it, he tears his hand away before it can even announce that his ride has been approved, and he pushes out through the opening door while the aircar is still thanking him and wishing him a nice day. He growls something under his breath in response.

Their door is decorated with an ugly painting of a guava tree. Linda, the 'foster mother,' is proud of this painting, which she painted herself. Paul thinks it is horribly disproportionate and that the guavas are a drab, ugly green.

It pops open before he can stick his thumb in the slot, and Linda's messy blond head sticks out. 'Hurry up, we're waiting for you,' she snarls. Paul can see Andrea's smug face behind her. Her eyes are sparkling.

Paul comes in to the sitting room to see everyone glaring at him. Tonya huffs a huge sigh. 'At last!' She tosses her braids back behind her head dramatically. Chan doesn't even say a word, he just leaps up and heads to the dining room.

Miki is the only one who smiles at him. But he's just five, he hasn't learned that people are horrible yet. Despite himself, Paul smiles back. He wishes he didn't care so much for the little tyke, but the kid has grown on him. Besides, someone has to be a responsible parent, and that sure isn't Linda.

He carefully puts his tablet and his other belongings away in his locker before he sits at the table. He remembers the last time he failed to do that, and Andrea uploaded a bunch of viruses on it.

He had to wipe it and reload everything, which meant he lost a library's worth of downloaded books, some of which he could not find again.

Hand sanitizer is passed along and Andrea jerks it out of his hands a couple of times before letting him have it. 'Now, now, stop that, Andrea dear,' Linda says absently as she settles in. Andrea is Linda's favourite. Paul passes it on to Miki, who says, 'Thank you.'

Linda meets their eyes in turn and raises her right hand. Paul and the others obediently follow suit.

'I thank the Founders for the gift of my survival,' they recite, 'and I thank the Hegemony for the generous gift of their bounty. I pledge my undying loyalty to the Hegemony in honour of the Founders. May they ever be remembered in gratitude.'

Paul has read in one of his books that crossing your fingers means that you do not really mean what you say when you make a promise. He is no longer naïve enough to believe that it is quite so simple, but he has not shaken the habit of keeping the fingers on his left hand crossed when swearing the Founders' Pledge.

The rations are carefully parcelled out onto their plates. Looks like a treat; spare ribs! No wonder no one wanted to wait! His mouth waters. The side dishes are squeezed out of their vacu-packs: rice and broccoli, with a side of canola oil.

There's even a dollop of barbecue sauce. Paul even knows why it's called that, because he knows what a barbecue was, at least by the descriptions. Everyone else thinks it's the name of an ancient country or something. He remembers asking whether they could have a barbecue once when he was small, but his mom explained that the air filtration system would be overly taxed by such a thing and they would be fined in rations if they tried it.

They eat their dinner in near-silence.

'So, have you made your appointment yet?' Linda asks him after a few minutes.

'Thursday, 15:00,' he grunts. He is too busy eating. Spare ribs are so rare! He savours every bite, carefully stripping the meat from the bones with his teeth one fibrous bit at a time. He even chews the gristle.

'We learned about the Last War today at school,' Tonya announces after shovelling her blended broccoli and rice into her face.

'What did you learn?' Linda asks after she finishes chewing.

'We learned how all the nations were fighting each other,' she gushes, pleased to have an audience that sounds interested. 'And how the Hegemony had to defend themselves against nukes and bio-war. Then we learned about the Liberal Rebellion. How they said they were against nukes but they took control of some nukes and some nuclear power plants and stuff, and how they threatened the Hegemony and the Hegemony had to take them down.'

Paul knows the lessons. They are repeated every year in the curriculum but there's something new added every time, some greater layer of complexity.

As the surface temperature and atmospheric carbon dioxide levels rose, and resources became more and more limited, the nations of the world began to compete for those resources. Eventually it erupted into a savage global free-for-all: the Last War.

The Hegemony formed to put a stop to the conflict by controlling all access to resources. It was necessary to make sure that everyone got an equal distribution, since people could not be trusted to manage themselves. As resources deteriorated further, it became necessary to allocate them according to need and societal value.

That's when the Liberal Rebellion began in earnest, eventually culminating in limited exchanges of nuclear and biochemical weapons that made much of the Surface uninhabitable – not that there was much left by then, anyway. The last act of the Founders was to form the Habitat.

'Some say that there's an underground Liberal movement starting up,' Andrea grins. Her eyes are bright. Is she, perhaps, imagining what she might do to the Liberals if they are caught?

Once he caught her with a rat she smuggled back to their living unit. She was amputating a limb while it was still conscious; he caught her because he was home earlier than usual and it was squealing. She was lashed five times for theft; which, he supposes, set the tone for their relationship from then on.

Linda lets her fork clatter to the plate. 'You stay away from whoever told you that!' she snaps. 'Either they're a liar and a troublemaker, or they're involved in something you don't want to be.'

Paul is more pleased than he should be at Andrea's squashed expression. She settles back into her chair and glowers. Well, good. He's certain she's full of shit anyway.

'Don't forget to select something to read from Doctrine after supper,' Linda reminds them as starts wiping down their plates and putting them away.

They all sit down to their tablets. Chan is reading Burke's 'Reflections on the Revolution in France,' while Tonya is listening to an audio-file of one of the approved novels. Miki is too young for such things so he's watching some archived cartoons that are recommended for children.

Paul is finally reading Ayn Rand. He's been avoiding it because of the name. All his life he's been asked, 'Any relation?' To his knowledge, the answer is no, though he has claimed one occasionally when it has been to his advantage.

'The first right on earth is the right of the ego. Man's first duty is to himself. His moral law is never to place his prime goal within the persons of others. His moral obligation is to do what he wishes, provided his wish does not depend primarily upon other men. This includes the whole sphere of his creative faculty, his thinking, his work. But it does not include the sphere of the gangster, the altruist and the dictator.'

What constitutes a dictator, he wonders? Does the Hegemony qualify? Or does being a group make them exempt?

'Hey; good luck on Thursday,' Chan whispers. Andrea grins at him. His heart sinks.

Assessment

Paul is sitting in the waiting room, slouched in an uncomfortable plastic chair. Everything is green: the walls are pale green, the chairs are dark green, the floor tiles are pea-green. He's trying to read but the words aren't sticking. There are three other kids in the room with him. None of them are looking at each other.

The first of the girls is called in. The door closes.

Thankfully, it's almost over. The aptitude tests have taken hours. *Answer these questions as quickly as you can. – Explain in a 500-word essay what field you think you would be best suited to and why? – Please press the button to signal when you hear the sound. – This game will measure your twitch reflexes, mental acuity, and ability to process visual and auditory information; please complete it as fast as you can. – Can you identify this scent? – What do you see in this inkblot image? – Write a 1000-word review of your favourite books from Doctrine, explaining why it is your favourite.* Paul chose *Starship Troopers*, mostly because it was a cool science fiction story that appealed to his desire to have some bad guy to fight. What he said, however, was that he approved of the idea of being required to contribute to support society before one could participate in its governmental processes.

The next kid is called in. Paul waits but the first does not return. He supposes this is probably to protect everyone's privacy.

At last he is called. He follows the nurse into the doctor's office with more than a little trepidation. It is a tiny room with fluorescent lights, a medical stretcher, and another uncomfortable chair. Now he sits and waits again.

After several more minutes the doctor comes in. She is a hatchet-faced woman with iron-grey hair and flint-grey eyes. She casts a cold gaze over him, sizes him up. 'Paul Rand?'

'Yes, ma'am.'

'Well, get up on the scale.'

He obeys. He is weighed and measured – five foot seven, 63 kilograms – a little small he supposes. Blood pressure is taken, vials and vials of blood are drawn. A lot of personal questions are asked. It is a crime to lie to a doctor, especially during an Assessment, so he answers everything from whether he has ever had a zit on his nose to how often he masturbates. He is told to cough. He has never been so uncomfortable, except when the Gendarmerie questioned him after his mother's death.

'You can go,' the doctor says at last. 'Be ready to be called in for a follow-up in the next few days, depending on what your tests results reveal.'

'Thank you, doctor,' says Paul politely, even though she has not been so courteous, and only rigid self-control prevents him from scrambling from the room. He makes himself walk, and with his head high. He feels violated.

He stops by the red-light district before he goes back to the apartment. The garish fluorescence hurts his eyes, and the driving electronic music thrums through his bones and flesh like a tectonic rumble.

He watches the scantily-clad Entertainers and wonders whether they *like* the role they've been given. It is not something that has ever occurred to him before. He could ask for one if he wanted – sixteen is old enough for even that kind of entertainment – but because he can't be sure, he chooses not to. Instead he trades in two of his collected drink tickets for some whiskey and weaves his way back to the apartment.

Miki is up late, waiting for him. He is sleeping on the couch in the sitting room, and he blinks awake when Paul comes in. He says nothing, just reaches his arms out for a hug. Paul obliges him.

'You smell funny,' Miki informs him.

He nods. 'I've been drinking.'

'You don't drink.'

'Today I do.'

Miki pursed his lips. 'It was hard?'

Paul nods. 'Yeah, it was hard.'

'Why do they do it?' Miki blinks up at him, his dark eyes full of questions and innocence.

Paul thinks about it. 'Well,' he says, 'resources are limited. They want to make sure that resources are allocated where they need to go. That includes us. We need to be doing what we're best suited to do for the good of society.' But does he really believe it? He's not sure he does. It seems so arbitrary to him somehow.

Miki nods solemnly. 'Where do you think I'll be most useful, Paul?'

He considers it. 'You like to fix things. Maybe an Engineer. Or a Plumber.' Both are important jobs with a lot of prestige. Why not encourage the boy to dream?

Miki grins. 'That sounds nice,' he says.

Paul wraps an arm around him. 'C'mon, kiddo. Let's go to bed.' They go to Paul's room and Paul tucks him into his bunk. Sleeping next to Miki reassures him too.

Follow-Up

It is three days later when Paul's screen blips again. His heart skips a beat. It is the Medical Centre. He has indeed been summoned for follow-up.

He considers whether he ought to send a message to Linda to tell her where he has gone. But he decides that she doesn't care anyway so why should he bother? He slings his bag over his shoulder and makes his way to the Centre.

The receptionist blinks owlishly at him. 'Yes, Paul Rand. Please have a seat.'

Waiting again. Obediently he sits in the uncomfortable green chair and stares at the green walls. He doesn't even try to read this time.

It doesn't take long. He's called in to the same examining room. That same hatchet-faced doctor is there. 'Hello Paul,' she says reassuringly. But her eyes do not change at all, so Paul is not reassured. 'Please sit down.'

Paul sits warily. 'Yes, ma'am?'

The doctor sits also, crossing her legs in her green medical uniform. Paul is wearing citizen grey. 'As you have probably guessed, we did find something of interest in your exam. We are going to keep you for a few days, just to see if we can track it down.'

'What did you find?' Paul asks. His mouth is dry. Illness is a terrible thing in the Habitat, and certainly it has to be contained and dealt with quickly, but he doesn't *feel* sick . . .

'I'm afraid you'll have to come with us,' she says. 'We're admitting you for treatment.' The doctor nods to someone at the doorway and a burly orderly comes in. There is another one outside.

Paul stands up and brushes off his pants. 'I'm at your disposal, doctor,' he says, as if he has a choice. 'Will you please see that my foster mother is informed?' He doesn't care if she is, but Miki needs to know.

'Of course.'

They step into an aircar. It speeds past the Residential District, deeper into the Medical District than he's ever been before. He can't help but feel they're driving into the gullet of a great beast.

Eventually they arrive at an airlock. Now Paul starts to feel real fear. 'Is it something communicable?' he asks the silent doctor nervously.

The doctor purses her lips. 'We don't want to discuss it too broadly. We're concerned about the public reaction. But there is an issue and it needs further study.'

He shivers. 'I see the problem,' he says. He is old enough to remember the last Habitat riot. How could he forget? He was about Miki's age, maybe, or a little younger? His brother was missing when the alarm was sounded.

He remembers hiding in their apartment for three days with the locks engaged. His father told them to stay put and disappeared into the chaos, and commanded that they not open the door until they knew it was him. Strange noises came from outside in the corridor every now and then – sometimes laughter, sometimes screams. His mother cried silently.

They ran out of water on the second day and were drinking out of the commode's reservoir. Twice the power went out, and Paul knew they were sealed in and if the power didn't come back on, they would die there. When it was over, the Gendarmerie came and opened the door.

They never saw his father again.

No, they don't need a panic. Paul can indeed appreciate their position.

The doctor thumbprints the censor and the airlock pops open. They enter another corridor.

Admission

He is asked to strip and ushered into a decontamination room. Paul is really frightened now. He puts the mask on as requested and tolerates a miserable cycle of hot shower, decontaminant that smells like something industrial, and another hot shower. A man in a biohazard suit shaves his head and clips his nails. Then he is directed to follow a white line along the wall which takes him to a series of cells. He is assigned one – 333A – and the door closes behind him. It seals shut.

The cell contains a simple hospital bed and a small desk and computer unit fastened to the wall. The monitor is on and the image of the doctor is waiting for him.

'Paul Rand,' she says as he sits down on the uncomfortable green chair to match the green sheet and blanket. 'Your test results indicate that you carry a latent communicable blood infection. You will not yet have noticed any symptoms because it *is* latent. However, we will be checking your close associates for signs of the infection as well. And because it is communicable, and dangerous, we will be keeping you in quarantine until we're certain it's cured. This will be an indefinite period, and the course of treatment is long, so expect that you will be here a while. It will involve daily injections and a course of oral antibiotics. There will also be an elaborate treatment process that will begin with intravenous antibiotics and other medications. This will be applied for three days and a nurse and orderly will arrive to get that started shortly. Other medications may be used as needed. Do you have any questions as this point?'

Paul swallows past the lump in his throat. 'Can you check the little boy I live with, Miki, first? I let him sleep in my bunk last night.'

'Of course,' she says. This was the first suggestion of anything other than a mechanical recitation in her voice. 'We'll check him right away. Anything else?'

He shakes his head. 'No, ma'am.'

'All right, we'll get started then,' the doctor says, and the call blips off to display a green home screen.

He runs his hand over his newly bald head and sits on the edge of the hospital bed, on the one side where the railing has been lowered. He has been allowed to keep his tablet, so he starts running through his library. He has finished *Starship Troopers* and is looking for something else to read. He starts a new story about a planet where nobody owns any property. Much of it reminds him of the world he knows.

A few minutes later the door chimes, and another orderly and a nurse come in. They are pushing an IV drip on a stand.

'Hi Paul, I'm Angelo,' the nurse smiles reassuringly through his germ mask. Paul can tell that he's smiling because his eyes crinkle. 'I'll be your nurse today. Can you make a fist for me please?'

They strap the band on his arm and he makes a fist. The IV needle goes in easily. There are three bottles on the IV solution; saline, and two with medicine. 'We're going to give you a mild sedative,' Angelo explains as he checks the plastic hoses for air bubbles. 'The antibiotics can make you feel a little nauseous so it can help to sleep. You want anything?'

'Some music would be nice,' Paul says, so Angelo shows him where the music directory is on the computer, and gives him the password to hook his tablet into their system.

He feels a little better when he hears a recording of some ancient acoustic guitar playing over the speakers. He's a little melancholy because he has never heard the old wood sound imitated in plastic or metal. Suddenly he feels mellow and very sleepy.

'I'll leave you to it then,' says Angelo kindly when Paul yawns, and he and the orderly go and shut the door.

Paul lays down on the bed and it isn't long before he passes out. It's more than a mild sedative.

He remembers little of the next several days. The only thing he's certain of is that he's terribly sick. He remembers vomiting a lot. He thinks that once he even almost drowns in it. Another time there is pain, like burning or a thousand tiny needles, on the back of his hand.

The rest are incoherent flashes. Images that must be induced by whatever the drugs are they give him; flashes of colour and light that cause pain in his nerves. Spasms and seizures. People yelling things that sometimes make sense – 'Get me the benzodiazepine!' – and sometimes don't – 'What's that spider doing in here?'

When he finally comes out of it, he has a tube in his nose and he is wearing a diaper.

'We almost lost you there,' Angelo tells him as he blinks back into consciousness. 'How do you feel now?'

He opens his mouth to talk and chokes around the tube in his nose, which is running down his throat.

'Looks like you're better,' Angelo nods. 'Yeah, that's a pain, isn't it? But you've been out of it for a week. Bad reaction to the medication. We'll get that removed.' Paul realizes he's been hooked up to monitors and the IV is still in. The monitor is showing the number 97.

'Blood oxygen level,' explains Angelo, indicating a censor which is attached to Paul's finger. He's adding a bag to the IV unit now. 'You'll still have that when you wake up but not for long. You're going in for surgery to remove that tube. We'll talk when you wake up.' And once again he's out.

Lunch

It takes several more days to recover. Paul aches all over. Occasionally he has pins and needles that crawl all over his body. They hurt. He scratches at them until it makes his skin raw. His skin is already terribly dry and it bleeds. They make him stop and when he can't, they bandage up his fingers.

Faceless nurses and orderlies come in and out, taking his temperature, monitoring him. A few times he wakes up pouring sweat. Once he gets an erection for nearly eight hours that won't go away. It doesn't seem to be connected to anything.

'Normal,' Angelo assures him.

He has trouble walking for several days after that, but eventually he works his way around with a cane. After a couple of days of hauling himself around the room Angelo encourages him to go and meet with the other patients. He limps through the corridor, leaning on his IV tree.

There are seven other patients in an open common room. The room is illuminated with full-spectrum light rather than fluorescents, which surprises him. All of them are older teenagers, like himself. They are wearing hospital gowns and they have short-buzzed hair, like the fuzz growing back on the top of his own head.

They all look exhausted, except for a large boy who is pacing back and forth in front of the large screen that dominates one side of the room. It's running an old program from the Time Before, a comedy show about a war in some place called Korea. All Paul knows about Korea is that it was one of the places that launched a nuke – and was nuked in return – in the Last War.

'Hi!' says a blond girl who would be pretty if her face wasn't puffy and tired-looking. But she's in better shape than he is; she has no metal tree growing plastic-bag fruit.

'Hi,' he says in return, and he eases himself down onto the bench she's sitting on.

'I'm Joan,' she says.

'I'm Paul.'

'Nice to meet you.' She gives him a smile meant to be sunny, but it lacks lustre.

'Likewise,' he smiles back, knowing his to be just as tired. 'How are you doing?'

'Better now.' She indicates his metal companion. 'You just came out of hell I see.'

He shrugs. 'I guess I had a bad reaction to the meds.'

A black-haired boy on the other side of the table barks out a sharp laugh. 'Everyone has a bad reaction to the meds,' he says dryly, scratching at his hand. There's a scab there that might have been an IV mark at one point. 'They don't tell you that. They don't want to scare you.'

He shrugs again. He assumed as much. Clearly what they have is incredibly dangerous.

The boy studies him for a moment. Then he says, 'I'm Zak,' and extends his hand. Paul offers the opposite one to shake, since his right has the IV needle in it.

'Aiko,' a black-haired girl with intense green eyes says. She is the curviest girl Paul has ever seen outside of old TV shows saved from the Time Before. One might even call her *plump*. Her breasts seem enormous to him as they sway under her hospital gown. She is making a sculpture out of plastisand. He realizes he is staring and looks away, embarrassed.

'Kismet,' says a dark-haired girl with unusually brown skin who is reading something on her tablet. She looks up long enough to wave.

'Alice,' another girl says from behind the table. She is doing push-ups. Paul realizes that her arms are probably bigger around than his. She has a husky alto voice and those flexing arms are hairy. Hormone imbalance, he wonders? He doesn't ask though. That would be rude.

'I'm Lukas,' says a brown-skinned boy about Paul's size, who is trying to squeeze a vice designed to strengthen the hands, and not doing well. His hand is trembling ever-so-slightly.

'Kashif,' says a boy just a little bigger than himself, who is tall and thin, with long fingers. He looks awkward in his tallness too, like he might have just had a growth spurt. He is picking notes out absently on a guitar. He's pretty good at it too. He stops long enough to jerk his thumb in the direction of the pacing boy. 'That's Jacob. I'm not sure if he'll say hi himself or not. He's got the crazies right now.'

'Fuck you!' Jacob growls back at Kashif with clenched fists.

'You see what I'm saying,' Kashif says in a stage whisper.

'I just want *out* of this fucking place!' he roars. He picks up a table and throws it at the screen, which sparks and shuts down. He starts kicking the walls and throwing anything in reach as he screams incoherent obscenities. He is so out of his mind with rage that his eyes are bright red and bugging out, and foam is sputtering from the edge of his mouth.

So fast Paul almost thinks he's imagining it, two orderlies appear and pin Jacob to the ground. 'Get off me!' he roars, writhing like a fish. A third orderly materializes, and while the other two are holding him, he shoots Jacob up with something in a hypodermic. Within minutes he is near-comatose. They carry him away.

Paul's heart is racing. 'Does he do that often?'

Zak grins. 'Oh no,' he says. 'Just once or twice a day or so.'

Paul gapes openly. He has never seen such crazy behaviour!

Joan shrugs. 'It's the treatment, the doctor says. It involves steroids. That's part of what they give us in the injections.'

'That's got to be too much,' he reasons. Is that what's happened to Alice? 'How deadly is this illness anyway?'

'All they'll tell us is that it's really important that we keep taking the treatment, regardless of the side effects,' says Lukas, giving up on the hand vice. He offers Paul a thin smile. 'I have all kinds of joint and nerve issues because of it.' Now that Paul is looking closely, he sees that Lukas' hands are swollen. His fingers are puffy and the joints look red and irritated. 'They say that it will pass, but . . .'

'That looks like it hurts,' Paul says sympathetically.

'Yeah,' he sighs.

'Lunchtime,' announces Angelo with a sunny smile as he enters the common room.

The trays they're provided with impress Paul. Eggs, tomatoes, toast (with *jam!*) and cream soup. It must be one and a quarter times what the usual caloric ration would be. It is served with a small plastic cup that holds three colourful pills. One is amber, one is lemon-yellow, and one is white. They are all round and about the same size.

'What are these?' he asks Angelo, shaking the pills in their cup.

'Meds to help with your condition,' Angelo assures him.

The others down their pills with a cup full of some sugary purple drink made from a powdered mix. It seems like it's extra strong to Paul. He makes a face.

Paul finds that he is rather hungry and he eats his food quickly. He notices that most of the others do the same; the only exception is Lukas, who picks at it. 'Are you okay?' he asks the boy.

'They say some appetite disturbance is normal,' he says with a shrug. 'They tell me it will come back.'

There's even a plate of cookies afterwards. They disappear quickly. Even Lukas eats those.

'So, does everyone just sit around here and wait to get better?' Paul asks with a scowl. He finds he is scratching at the bandage over the IV. He makes himself stop.

'Pretty much,' says Kashif.

'Why, are you feeling like a ball of energy?' snaps Zak.

Paul shrugs. 'No. I just hate the idea of sitting around here cooped up.' He looks to where Alice is now doing sit-ups. 'I think Alice is a ball of energy.'

She stops exercising and looks back over at Paul, taking a moment to get her breath. 'Not really,' she pants. 'But with this treatment cycle, you put on weight. It's one of the major side effects. I'd rather be muscled than fat.' She glances over at Aiko, who raises her eyebrows at Alice and says nothing.

Paul can see her point. He remembers how people treated Matthew, a pudgy boy who was in his classes with him until last year. He used to get beat up and his lunch ration was stolen on a regular basis. 'I know you're stealing food from somewhere, fatty,' Andrea sneered at him, 'so you won't miss it.'

He remembers wondering whether she might be right. With rations so tightly controlled, where did one get enough food to put on that much weight anyhow? He researched it, and learned that all kinds of things could affect size besides the amount of food one ate. Such as time of day that one ate meals at, genetics, hormone imbalances, diabetes, and yes, medication.

Matthew had eventually stopped coming to class. The rumour was that he had taken his own life.

After lunch, the doctor arrives. She does not greet them, nor ask how any of them are feeling. She is accompanied by two very large orderlies. They are bigger than Alice. 'Time for weigh-in,' she announces.

As if they've done it many times before, they all line up to a scale that's on the far side of the room, which Paul hadn't paid much attention to when he came in. They are weighed in alphabetical order by last name. They are also measured, and more blood is drawn. Alice is the only one to follow him.

'72 kilograms,' Angelo announces when Aiko is weighed. She's about five foot five or six. *That* is *fat,* Paul thinks to himself. Alice isn't much lighter – 70 kilograms – but she's about Paul's height.

Paul finds to his dismay that he has gained six kilograms while unconscious. No wonder his limbs feel heavy.

'Could be water weight from the saline,' Angelo reassures him with a friendly smile. 'It all goes away after treatment.'

Paul is beginning to not like Angelo's smile. What is he hiding?

Messages

After the doctor leaves, Paul tries to get to know some of the others. It's difficult. They don't really want to talk, and there are always orderlies around so it's hard to get privacy.

After a while he gives up and starts trying to read again. But he's having trouble concentrating. He finds that he is drowsy, and he ends up napping for a few minutes in a chair.

Half-awake, for just a moment he thinks he sees a message screen on his tablet. There's just one word: 'BEWARE.' He blinks and it disappears; if it ever was there in the first place. As he rubs the sleep from his eyes, he realizes he must be imagining it. Obviously, he is frightened and anxious, and what with the hallucinations he suffered when he was unconscious, his mind must still be fighting off traces of the drug and projecting his fears.

He checks through his message history to be sure, but it's empty. That bothers him. He hardly expects protests from the foster home, but surely at least Miki should have sent him something!

But, he realizes, *I have some kind of disease. Something so awful they won't tell me what it is. Maybe he doesn't want to talk to me. Maybe he's afraid.*

The thought makes him feel melancholy. To be honest, he is downright depressed. He tries to focus on his book again, but he has no more luck than before.

One of the orderlies appears again. He has a drink tray full of thick, foamy white drinks.

Certain that they have just eaten, Paul glances at the clock on his tablet, and is startled to realize that two hours have passed. How long has he been sleeping?

The kids all take them. Paul samples his. It's sweet-tasting again. He thinks it's probably made from rice milk and bananas. There's a malty taste to it as well. Tasty! 'What is this?' he asks no one in particular.

'Got to keep our blood sugar up,' says Joan. 'The meds can lead to low blood sugar too, and that's one of the reasons weight gain is a side effect. We get these between meals.'

Paul doesn't think he'll have room for the thick, frothy drink after that big lunch, but he's wrong. He finishes it before he realizes it.

They play games in the evening, or zone out on the screen. Paul tries to get involved in a game of chess with Aiko, but he just can't concentrate. Eventually he gives up and watches the news. It's all a propaganda piece against insurgents. Paul doubts they exist. Maybe they did once, but they were caught a long time ago. Which is why he no longer has a mother.

Supper is served. It's a thick vegetable stew. Again, Paul finds that he's unusually hungry and he eats it all, despite feeling overstuffed afterwards.

After that, the routine is quiet time. Paul starts getting into reading again, but Lukas sits down next to him. 'You like to read?' he asks.

Paul shrugs. 'I like science fiction from the Time Before.'

'Why?'

'Dunno. I think it's because I like to think about what people thought the world was going to be like. I guess maybe because I hope there might be some clue in it to help make this one better. I suppose that probably sounds stupid,' he adds hastily, not wanting to give such a sentiment any public weight. That might be interpreted badly.

'Nah,' says Lukas. 'I can't see how hope can hurt.' He picks at his nails for a minute. The skin around them is flaking.

But Paul doesn't agree. He knows that hope *can* hurt. A lot. 'Want to play some chess?'

'Sure,' says Lukas, and they get a game going, despite Paul's lack of interest.

The game is well underway, and he is moving his knight to box in Lukas' queen when he gets the feeling that someone is watching him. He looks up. Aiko is looking back. She blushes, and looks away. He watches her breasts sway as she turns and heat flares in his belly, and a little lower too. *Do they lock the rooms at night?* he wonders. *Would she mind if I came over and said hi?*

The thought embarrasses him. He's never had much interest in sex. The truth is, he has no desire to start relationships, and he wouldn't feel right about something more casual. Maybe it's because he doesn't trust people. He doesn't even like them much.

'Lights out,' says Angelo when 20:00 rolls around. Paul gets up and stretches. 'Good game,' he tells Lukas. 'I guess you won, since you've got more pieces left than I do.'

'Nah, leave it,' he says. 'We can pick it up in the morning.'

'Good night!' Aiko says to him, casting him a radiant smile.

He meets her eyes. 'See you later,' he promises. She makes a poor attempt to wink. *All right then,* he thinks to himself, excitement building in his belly. How closely do they monitor the systems at night, he wonders? 'Night, Lukas,' he says offhandedly, and everyone heads off, presumably to their rooms. He goes back to 333A.

Another nurse, not Angelo, is waiting for him. 'Hi Paul, I'm Marcie,' she says with a smile. He dislikes that smile instantly. It's a saccharine smile, full of false sweetness, like the powdered drink mix. She's another large person. Do they select for big, muscled people for jobs at this facility? 'I'm here to take your blood pressure and blood oxygen levels, and to give you your evening medications.'

'Sure,' he says absently, still thinking about Aiko and her phony wink. He is asked to make a fist and then a blood pressure cuff is applied and tightened.

'120 over 80,' she announces after a moment. 'Perfectly normal.'

'That's a little high for me,' he points out. 'My last was 110 over 70. It should be in my chart. That was only . . .' He cuts himself off because he realizes that he doesn't have the information required to complete the sentence. 'How long have I been here, anyway?'

'You don't need to worry about that,' Marcie the Night Nurse chides him gently as she removes the cuff. Then she prepares a gleaming hypodermic, which she injects into the IV. 'There you are, that ought to fix things up for you. Have a good sleep!' She heads out and the door shuts.

He decides he's going to get into bed and play around on his tablet until the lights go out, so that he can sneak out with less likelihood of being detected. He fires it up and this time, he sees a message that says, 'DON'T TAKE THE PILLS.' It disappears almost immediately, so fast he almost can't comprehend what it said. Did he really see it?

This time he decides that he did. It isn't something he is likely to imagine; it's too weird for that! Someone has obviously hacked his system. But when he checks back again, there is no evidence that it was ever present.

A wave of exhaustion hits him suddenly. Just like that, he can barely keep his eyes open. *There was a sleeping drug in that needle,* he realizes, just before the green darkness swallows him.

Bitter Pills

Morning starts off pretty much the same way. When he wakes up, Paul is so foggy that he can't remember why he was upset as he was going to sleep. He tries to shake off the exhaustion as breakfast is served. It's a thick porridge, and there's as much of it as they want to eat. It seems to him that they eat quite a bit of it, except for Lukas, whose appetite is still poor. Paul does not have that problem, and the food is so good, that once again he eats until his belly hurts.

'Time for daily exercise,' Angelo announces. They are led in a series of low -impact exercises 'because your joints are sensitive with your condition,' Angelo explains. Yoga and qi gong, mostly. Paul feels that the exercise is good for him and helps to stretch his muscles and clear his head. But he can't help but notice that Jacob is nowhere to be seen.

'Where's Jacob?' he asks Angelo bluntly when they come in with some more of those blended foamy drinks.

'He's not feeling that great,' Angelo replies; with, Paul now notices, just the right note of cheerfulness and regret. It would probably fool almost anyone else, but Paul knows what to look for and his hackles immediately raise. 'He's going to have to receive some extra treatment in isolation for a while.'

Is he telling the truth? Paul thinks that it *sounds* truthful. But he also notices that Angelo keeps his eyes straight forward, in an almost glassy manner like a stuffed toy, and that tells Paul that he's hiding things as well. Skills that he learned from his parents when he was still small.

'I'm sorry to hear it,' says Paul sincerely.

Some time is allotted for screens or reading after that. Paul wants to go online, but he is unsurprised to learn that this is forbidden here. 'It's important that you concentrate on your recovery,' Angelo says by way of excuse. Paul doesn't believe a word of it. There is something very wrong here.

Afterwards, lunch again, this time fried eggs on toast with tomato soup. Not until Paul sees the little cup of pills does he remember the message he thought he saw on his tablet.

He glances around. Yes, it seems like Angelo and the orderlies are watching everyone carefully. Are they trying to make sure that they all take the meds? How is he going manage this?

His eye catches on Kismet, who is watching him. Having made eye contact, she tips back the cup into her mouth. Her tongue works and he think he sees a small bump at the side of her mouth, next to her molars. That side of her face is turned away from the orderlies. She takes a gulp of the drink mix – orange this time – and swallows visibly. The pills are worked out from around her teeth with her tongue and spat into the cup, which she takes in her left hand.

As she starts eating with her right hand, under the table the hand holding the cup tips the slightly-dissolved pills into her palm. She crushes them up in her palm and starts to allow some of the dust to sprinkle onto the floor. Some is brushed under her gown, and then she returns the cup to the table. She drinks more of the sugary drink, then, as if by accident, holds it in her lap, where she deposits the rest of the ground-up pills.

Paul watches this whole performance out of the corner of his eye, while pretending to eat. He sees the logic of smearing the pill powder on her body. It will get caught in her body hair, and it will slowly fall off in bits and pieces, instead of all at once. Far less likely to be detected.

He makes a snap decision to follow suit, and, used to making hand motions out of sight of authorities, he breaks up and disperses his own pills. Not as deft as she is, he feigns being done with eating while there's still some food on the plate – which is a lie, he's still hungry, and he finds it takes an amazing amount of willpower to leave even a morsel – and conceals the bulk of the medication in the remains of his tomato soup, where rice milk camouflages it. His mouth burns from where the pills touched his gums. There is a horribly bitter taste in his mouth.

Quickly Paul glances to Kismet again. She smiles a little at the corners of her mouth. Then she looks away. But Paul is suddenly much happier. Whatever is going on, he is no longer alone.

That afternoon he finds that he has much more energy than he did the day before. He decides to join Alice in push-ups and sit-ups. She nods appreciatively at him and they work out together. If he must choose between fat and muscle, he'd rather choose muscle too. They work up a good sweat.

A couple of weeks pass, with little variation in the routine. Paul waits hopefully for more communications, some sign from Kismet, another message flashing across his screen, and nothing happens.

Nor does he get any closer to deciphering the mystery of their situation. He knows better than to ask questions. The last time he did such a thing, before he was admitted, he found himself under bright white lights for three days while an endless rotation of officers asked him the same questions over and over. He wasn't even allowed to eat, although one of the cops made a mistake and left a banana from his lunch, which he devoured before they could stop him.

Without the pills, he finds that his appetite quickly deteriorates. It's easy to hide the pills because he doesn't want the food. His weight drops, and so does Lukas' weight. Kismet's and Zak's don't change much at all. Everyone else gains at a steady, and alarmingly rapid, rate. Kashif starts to fill out on that long, lanky frame, and Aiko becomes ever more freakish-looking to eyes accustomed to thin, sometimes even gaunt, faces.

But Angelo is not stupid, and he catches that something is up with Paul. He starts watching him closely enough while he's eating that he has no choice but to swallow the pills.

The correlation is apparent immediately. That afternoon he dozes off in a green faux-leather common room chair again, watching some old TV show about ghosts and a bumbling troupe of fools who have to stop them with nuclear accelerators, which they can wear on their backs in heavy backpacks, shoot glowing green beams of light, and somehow manage not to irradiate themselves or every person and place they come in contact with. He's sure he must be watching the same show, but it turns out he has dozed through a marathon.

As he comes to for their evening shake, he thinks he sees a brief message flash across his screen again. This time it says, 'BE MORE CAREFUL OR THEY'LL FORCE FEED THEM TO YOU.'

He is both excited and frightened, but his head is far too fuzzy to contemplate this development with the focus it deserves. Paul nods for most of the evening as well.

The following day he wakes up ravenously hungry again.

Once again at lunch he's required to swallow the pills under Angelo's dark-eyed supervision. But right after weigh-in, which is his earliest opportunity, he sneaks into the bathroom and forces himself to vomit the pills back up, along with most of his lunch. It feels like it's burning his lungs when it comes back out, but it's just his esophagus. He pukes silently and quickly so he won't be detected. The pain is like being on fire.

It's half a victory. He's still drowsy in the afternoon, but not like when he takes a full dose. This time he decides to pretend he's more exhausted than he is. Out of the corner of a partially-cracked eyelid he sees Angelo approach him and wave hands in front of his face. When he doesn't react, the nurse nods and smiles, and goes about his work, cleaning up after all the dozing kids.

Paul is beginning to think they aren't dozing. He's starting to think they're all stoned out of their minds.

He wonders why it is that he only seems to be seeing the messages when he's just waking up? The only reason he can think of is a strong argument against their reality. They must be hallucinations induced by whatever crazy drugs they're being given. That's certainly the most logical explanation!

But he knows a thing or two about computers that the average person doesn't know. One thing that he's aware of is that any screen is also capable of being a camera. What if They (whoever They are; who's in charge here, anyway?) can *tell* if you're reading your screen? Will this send an automatic signal to some mainframe somewhere to record a screenshot?

That system might be fooled by the moment between waking and sleeping, when you look at things in the waking world without really seeing them. And perhaps that gives someone just a split second to send a message; but only that, and no more.

He decides to test the theory. He zones out on the screen through cracked eyelids, like a fortune teller gazing at a crystal ball. *Tell me the future,* he urges it.

A message does appear. 'GOOD JOB,' it says. 'NOW PRETEND YOU'RE STILL TAKING THE DRUGS.' It startles him out of his meditation and the message goes away.

Yes; in order to delude the hospital staff, especially sharp-eyed Angelo, he will have to break or vomit up the drugs as he can, and dispose of the rest a lot more carefully than he is doing. Paul knows he will also have to fake the symptoms of the medication, which includes sleeping away most of the afternoon and eating a ridiculous amount of food. Plus, whatever is in those shakes.

No wonder Aiko is getting fat. It's surprising that no one else is, really. Not yet, anyway.

The next morning, he is hungry but not ravenous. He stuffs himself anyway, and catches Angelo's secret smile. It's like the smile of a trapper who knows that a rat is stepping into his spring-triggered cage. He bites down on the anger that is burning in his belly.

Thorazine

Over the next couple of weeks, Paul realizes he is going through a growth spurt. The bar on the ruler starts shifting up in increments. He has not grown so much at once since he was a child. Five-seven, five-eight, five-nine, and over a period of another three weeks. At least, that's how long he thinks it's been because he's started checking off the days on a bar on his tablet. There are no clocks, save the one on his tablet, and no contact with the world outside. He could have been here for a day or a thousand years.

It's awful. His legs and joints ache all the time. He would expect that the excruciating pain that returns to him every morning would wake him in the middle of the night, like growing pains used to.

But it takes him several days to realize it's suspicious that it doesn't. He concludes they are injecting him with a tranquilizer of some kind, though the IV is long gone now and this is a direct needle to the bloodstream. They offer him painkillers, but he refuses. He feels he already has too many drugs in his system.

On top of this, he can't stop thinking about sex, and he gets erections from the most insignificant of things. His hospital gown brushes him wrong and pop! It's humiliating. Or it would be, except that most of them seem too stoned to care, except Aiko, whose expression is impossible to mistake. She licks her lips when he meets his gaze. Maybe the meds are affecting her in the same way.

Those amazing breasts seem even bigger to him. Come to think of it, he is almost certain that all the girls' breasts are bigger. He considers it at length one day, and he realizes with a start that even Kismet, who was flat-chested when he arrived save for little budding nubs, has to have a B cup by now. Alice too.

While he's on the subject, he realizes his nipples seem a little swollen. And they *hurt* when touched by anything. Fear bolts through him at this realization. What is *happening* to all of them? What is happening to his body?

There's more. He starts putting on weight as well. He is bulking up like Alice. His shoulders are getting broader and the scale tells him he weighs 70.5 kilograms now. He has red stretch marks under his armpits. He needs to shave daily, and his voice is cracking for the second time in his life.

He keeps hoping something else will appear on the tablet message system, but nothing does. He starts trying to explore things that he doesn't normally dig into on his tablet. He's no hacker, but he knows a few tricks that his father and brother taught him. Perhaps the person trying to communicate with him has left a code somewhere for him to find. It occurs to him that science fiction novels are the most likely place for anyone who knows anything about him to do that. He starts combing through them, looking for anything out of the ordinary.

He finally finds it, but it's subtle. Extra characters have been added to words in the files. For instance, in an old sci-fi horror novel about a child with the power to start fires with her mind, there is a series of odd characters next to the word 'Thorazine.' The evil government agents shoot the girl's father with a tranquilizer dart that uses it.

Paul freezes where he is sitting, and it takes a moment of conscious work to wipe the stunned realization from his face. A made-up word from another novel he read comes to mind; *tharn*. It is used to describe the paralyzing fear and stupefaction that freezes rabbits exposed to bright headlights on a dark road. Yes, the thought makes him *tharn*.

It's *Thorazine* they're shooting him up with. He's certain of it. Reading more about the drug in the story, he learns it's an antipsychotic and a tranquilizer, and he's sure he remembers hearing somewhere that normal people who take anti-psychotics are completely messed up by them. Which could explain his occasional hallucinations. And it also increases appetite and saps energy; the child's father in the story puts on weight after it is given to him for a few months regularly.

Why in the hell are they giving us Thorazine? his frantic brain tries to determine. It is running around in a panic loop. *We're not patients; we're* prisoners*!*

He memorizes that stream of characters and starts trying it in different places. He tries saving files with that name, and that doesn't work. He types it into documents. He tries adding it in hidden paths in his bios. Nothing.

Finally, he types 'Thorazine' into his message app, and he sends it off to the string of characters.

A few minutes later, the reply comes back, 'WHAT TOOK YOU SO LONG?'

Paul just about laughs out loud, he is so relieved. 'TOO STONED TO THINK,' he replies. His eyes meet Kismet's. Hers are glittering and there is an almost imperceptible nod when they connect with his.

'BE CAREFUL,' Kismet cautions. 'THEY WON'T BE ABLE TO EVESDROP ON THE CONVO NOW, BUT THEY CAN STILL WATCH & READ WHAT YOU TYPE OVER YOUR SHOULDER.'

'RIGHT,' he sends back. A quick glance tells him that no one is currently watching, but he makes sure his tablet is ensconced in his lap so the cameras can't pick it up.

'CAN'T AVOID THE INJECTIONS,' she types. 'THEY'LL FORCE THEM ON YOU IF YOU ARGUE. JACOB WAS BEAT BADLY AT ONE POINT.'

'WHAT IS GOING ON HERE?' he demands. 'WHY ARE THEY GIVING US THORAZINE? WHAT'S IN THOSE INJECTIONS?'

'WE CAN'T BE SURE,' she taps back, 'BUT WE THINK IT'S A SOUP OF STEROIDS AND HUMAN GROWTH HORMONE.' Her mouth is a tight, think line.

Human growth hormone? That explains the growth spurt, doesn't it? And the hormonal weirdness too. And the steroids explain the bulking up, and the irritability and rage, especially in combination.

'GOT TO STOP THIS NOW. THEY GET SUSPICIOUS IF WE TYPE TOO FAST AND IT SOUNDS CONNECTED.' She cuts the message window off abruptly.

Paul quickly opens a document window and starts typing nonsense. Doggerel from his childhood. Little Miss Muffet. The

Old Woman in the Shoe. But in the meantime, his mind is working, racing over the issue.

Steroids he can understand. If there's a latent issue that causes tissue damage, steroids seem a sensible treatment. Prednisone, maybe, or cortisol injections. But the symptoms are more like those of anabolic steroids. He knows this because some of his old novels talk about super-soldiers.

But *human growth hormone?* What can that possibly be for?

Angelo passes by and, just casually, glances at his tablet. 'Nursery rhymes?' he asks with a curious expression.

'Miki and I used to like them.' This is true, though this was a year or so back now. 'I'm trying to think of any I might have forgotten. They're hard to find in the archives.' That's not a lie either.

Angelo nods. 'Makes sense,' he agrees. 'I'm sure you'll see him soon.' He moves on.

Paul's fist curls under the table and for just a moment, he clearly visualizes choking Angelo to death in his green gown. Sweat beads his brow. He makes himself look away.

Hansel and Gretel

There's no more opportunity to message for the rest of the day. He begins to feign becoming accustomed to the meds and does a little light exercise in the afternoon before 'dozing' again. His mind is a spinning wheel. He's so anxious that his heart is thumping in his ears, and it shows in his evening blood pressure reading. 190 over 90,

'That's a sudden jump,' observes Marcie.

'I've heard some things about this condition we're supposed to have,' he explains truthfully, 'and it's scaring the shit out of me.'

'What have you heard?' she asks, a little too nonchalant.

'Nothing specific, and maybe that's worse,' he says. Again, truth, if a bit misleading.

She gives him that sickly-sweet reassuring smile that he doesn't trust. 'Don't you worry, Paul. Everything works out in the end.' She pats his hand before she shoots him up with her witches' brew.

Knowing he has only moments before he passes out, he opens the message window and types, 'IF YOU KNOW WHAT'S GOING ON, PLEASE TELL ME.' He shuts it down immediately without waiting for the reply, aware that he will likely slip into unconsciousness before he gets it, and this turns out to be a wise decision, because he barely remembers doing so.

'So, are we all sixteen?' Joan wonders the next morning over another large breakfast. Paul has started cutting down now. More 'adaptations to the medication.'

Paul thinks about it. That would be very odd indeed.

'I think so,' Aiko shrugs. 'They turned up the illness in my Assessment.'

Paul stares at her for a minute. 'So why is there no one here whose condition was discovered when they had their basic yearly physical?' He could understand separating kids and adults, but why no variation in their ages? Were there so many people with the illness that they were *separating* them by age?

That would be catastrophic. The Habitat can't afford to sustain such losses, and he doubts the other Habitats could either.

He fires up his tablet as soon as he can. The answer is not promising. 'WE HAVE SUSPICIONS BUT WE DON'T KNOW FOR SURE. I'M NOT SURE I WANT TO.'

Hope for an organized resistance flares briefly when she says 'we,' but the last dashes them. 'WHO ARE "WE"?'

'ME ZAK KASHIF. WE WANT TO RECRUIT ALICE BUT WE THINK SHE'S TOO FAR GONE.'

He glances over at Alice, who is vigorously working out now, and is rapidly sculpting herself into an Amazonian statue. Sexy. He shakes his head. He has more important things to think about. 'I THINK IT'S WORTH A SHOT. BUT RECRUIT FOR WHAT?' he asks.

'ESCAPE,' she taps back immediately. 'THEY'RE LOOKING AT US.'

He starts working on nursery rhymes again, but is drawing a blank. Perhaps he should move on to what he can recall of fairy tales.

'Hey Alice,' he says, struck with a sudden inspiration, 'Come here for a minute, would you?'

Alice snaps her gaze over from the leg lifts. 'What?' she growls as she wipes the sweat from her brow. When he doesn't immediately respond, she sighs and starts making her way over.

'I'm making a list of fairy tales and nursery rhymes for this little kid I live with,' he explains when she's about halfway over so she can't change her mind. 'Can you look at it for me and see if you can't think of something I might have missed?'

'Why me?" she complains. 'I don't know anything about fairy tales.' But she has a look anyway, and carefully, out of view of the cameras (the ones he knows about anyhow) he shows her the conversation.

She meets his eyes. 'Sure, I can think of one,' she says. 'The Minotaur of Minos'

'That's not a fairy tale, that's a myth,' Joan points out reasonably.

'Is it?' she says absently. 'My mistake.' But she meets Paul's eyes, and he knows it's no mistake. 'Why don't you come work out with me? You look like you're feeling better today.' She pokes him in the ribs. 'And you're getting soft.'

He thinks she's probably right. He's up to 73 kilograms now. Getting a bit pudgy. 'Sure,' he says happily, killing the chat windows but leaving the document up.

Lunch is served not long after. Then it's time for weigh-in. This time, Paul watches everything with an eye to tactics. The two assistant orderlies are covering the exits while Angelo and the doctor see to the weighing and the measuring. It's obvious, now that he's looking for it. He has learned to dispose of the ground-up pills when everyone is distracted with this process.

Everyone has put on weight now, even Lukas, whose appetite has returned. 'You need to slow down on the exercise, I think,' says the doctor to Alice. 'It's not good for your joints.'

'I'll try and do that,' she says. Paul can see that her hands are trembling. Exhaustion? Rage?

'Up on the scale, Aiko,' the doctor commands. Aiko waddles up to the scale and waits.

'75 kilograms,' announces Angelo.

'Oh dear,' says Aiko sadly.

The doctor looks her over. Paul doesn't like something in that assessing look. It's like someone checking over a part to see if it's suitable for work or if it ought to be rejected. She grips Aiko's face and turns it from side to side. Then she pinches her cheeks.

'I think you're ready, my dear,' she says.

Ready for what? Paul wonders. Alarm bells start going off in his head. *'Ready?' Why not 'better'?*

But Aiko misses the subtle connotation. Either that, or he's reading things into it that he shouldn't be. He supposes he could be paranoid. They are, after all, giving him drugs that cause paranoia as a side effect.

Her round face lights up. 'I can go home now?' she asks hopefully.

'Yes, I think it's time for you to be discharged,' says the doctor with a thin-lipped smile.

Cheers and applause erupt. Even Alice, even Paul congratulates her. Aiko is so happy that tears leak out of her eyes. She thanks the doctor for her care, and Angelo for his concern. She is taken from the room and down the hall, with one of the orderlies trailing behind her. There is only one orderly now, guarding the door she left through, and Angelo.

'I've got a fairy tale you forgot,' Alice says to him as soon as they're gone. Her breathing, he notes suddenly, is shallow, and her hands are clenching and unclenching. He forces himself not to look at the orderly to see if he has noticed.

'What's that?' he asks her.

She clears her throat. 'Hansel and Gretel,' she whispers. Her eyes are wide and the pupils fully dilated. He realizes it's not anger he sees in her face and body language; it's *fear*.

Then what she said hits him.

Tharn. Again, he is almost *tharn*. But he looks to Alice and to Kismet and this gives him courage. Without stopping to consider the wisdom of it, or the consequences, he throws himself at Angelo and knocks him down.

Alice does not miss her signal. She lets out an animal roar and bashes the orderly in the side of the head with an elbow.

To their credit, Kismet, Zak and Kashif are up on their feet immediately. But they are not fighters. They hesitate, uncertain of what to do, or what is going on.

Paul, however, is. His parents, who were insurgents in the underground Liberal Movement, have trained him in combat arts. He is slow from the enforced lax physical regime, but he knows how to kill with his hands, though he has never had to use it. He makes a knuckle with his fist and drives it into Angelo's throat, crushing or at least severely damaging his windpipe.

He falls and lays there, gasping. Paul rifles through his clothing. He finds a hypodermic needle and, as he expects, a 45 semi-automatic in a concealed holster. 'They're armed!' he cries, just as he hears a gunshot go off.

He does not waste limited ammunition. Instead he stomps hard on Angelo's throat and crushes it. 'Fucking SADIST!' he roars, and his vision goes red at the edges. He fights to get a grip on himself. *It's the steroids and the hormones,* he assures himself, *and if you do not calm down, you will die.*

He turns his gaze to the others. Joan is lying on the floor, blood pouring from her belly and mouth, and it looks like she is trying to hold it in with her hands but it's getting away.

The orderly is struggling against Alice and Zak, who are sitting on him. Kismet is aiming the gun in his direction but she has no idea what she's doing. Her hand is shaking. Lukas is brandishing a green chair above his head with trembling arms, waiting to smash somebody with it.

Paul walks up to the orderly, snaps the magazine back on the pistol, then puts the barrel to his temple and pulls the trigger. His head deflates and blood and ooze sags out of the side of it.

'Oh my God!' shrieks Kismet, and she starts to cry. From somewhere far away, Joan is moaning.

'No,' he says, as alarms sound and steel cages begin to slam down on all the exits. He jerks her arm. 'No, we have only one hope, and that's you. If you can keep our messages from their spybots, you must have a line out to the internet. Do you?'

She wipes the tears out of her face with a shaking hand. 'Yes, I do,' she says in a tiny voice.

'Then start a feed up, and broadcast whatever you can. Do it now.'

Obediently she starts working the keys. Alice takes the gun.

Armed men crowd the exits. They are wearing full suits of tactical body armour and they are armed with rifles. Paul knows how this must end. 'Do it quickly,' he whispers. He puts his body between her and the soldiers of the Gendarmerie.

The soldiers part like the Red Sea of yore to make way for the doctor. 'Paul,' she sighs, 'can we talk about this?'

'Why?' he demands, stalling for a few minutes of precious time. For Aiko, and Joan, and Kismet. For his brother Jamie. For all of them. 'I thought you had to have a genetic flaw.'

'You do have one,' she says. 'You're a carrier for Huntington's Disease. You won't get it, but your children might.'

He can't believe what he's hearing. His hands go up to his temples of their own accord. 'We've had the genetic engineering technology to fix that for more than a century!'

She smiles. It is a bloody knife slash across her face. 'We have to make the decision somehow.'

'All of us?' asks Zak in a small voice.

She nods. 'It will be easier if you just come quietly. There's no way you can escape anyway.'

Paul shakes his head in disbelief. 'This is what we've come to? Our population is so decimated that even *correctable* genetic conditions are selected? What about the other Habitats?'

'*What* other Habitats?' demands the doctor with an eerie laugh. 'Ever since the Bean Rot got out of control and killed all the legumes, we haven't had enough sources of complex protein. Chickens and rats can only take us so far. We had to do *something*.'

'WHAT IS SHE TALKING ABOUT?!' shrieks Kismet at the top of her lungs, as the realization sinks in.

Alice bleats out a bitter laugh. 'Where in the hell did you think spare ribs came from? Cows and pigs have been extinct for a hundred years!'

'Oh, God,' she moans, the tablet dropping from her hands. 'Oh my God!' She immediately vomits up her lunch.

'Zak,' he says, and Zak takes the tablet.

'Drop that,' hisses the doctor, 'or my men will shoot you.'

'We're going to die anyway,' Zak snaps back. He looks to the screen.

Paul raises the pistol. 'Not before I shoot you, doctor.' He is proud of the even tone of his voice.

She laughs. 'You can't shoot all of them at once!' But it has a nervous, metallic edge to it.

'I'm not going to shoot them all. Just you.'

'We got it!' Zak laughs. 'She did it! The upload is finished!'

Paul sags in relief. 'It's over, doctor,' he sighs. 'The whole Habitat knows what you've done now.'

She screams her laughter out loud. 'Do you really think they're going to *care*? Would you have cared? You were happy enough to be part of it when it wasn't you, weren't you, Paul? It's not in their interests! It's food on their table!'

She might be right, Paul realizes.

He pulls the trigger.

About the Author

Diane Morrison lives with her partners and works part-time in a bookstore in Vernon, BC, where she was born and raised. An avid National Novel Writing Month participant, she is proudly Canadian and proudly LGBTQ. Under her pen name 'Sable Aradia' she is a successful Pagan author, a musician, and a professional blogger. After a lifetime of putting the needs of her family first, she is striking out to become what she always wanted to be; a speculative fiction writer.

Other Books by Diane Morrison

The Wyrd West Chronicles

Showdown

Vice & Virtue

The Vigil

Chasing Fireflies: A Summer Romance Anthology (Contributor)

As Sable Aradia

The Witch's Eight Paths of Power: A Complete Guide to Magick and Witchcraft

Pagan Consent Culture (Contributor)

The Pagan Leadership Anthology (Contributor)

www.ingramcontent.com/pod-product-compliance
Lightning Source LLC
Chambersburg PA
CBHW020313150626
46552CB00022B/2867